EGMONT
We bring stories to life

First published in Great Britain 2011
by Egmont UK Limited,
239 Kensington High Street, London, W8 6SA

Editor: Catherine Such
Art Editor: Amanda Hartley
Editorial Assistant: Hannah Greenfield
Group Editor: Keilly Swift
Group Art Editor: Jeanette Ryall

ISBN 978 1 4052 5687 2
1 3 5 7 9 10 8 6 4 2

Printed in Italy

Adult supervision is recommended when glue, paint,
scissors and other sharp points are in use.

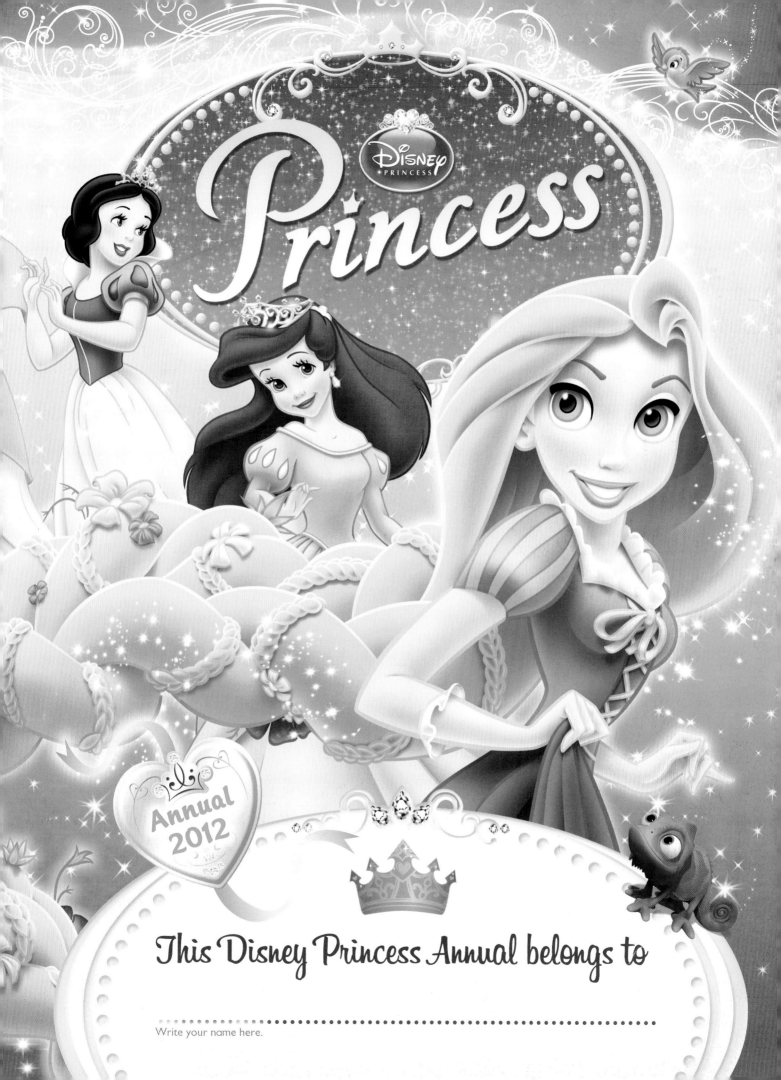

Princess

Annual 2012

This Disney Princess Annual belongs to

Write your name here.

Disney Princess

All this inside ...

Part 5

Aurora

Part 6

Jasmine

Part 7

Belle

Part 8

Snow White

Learn how to be a princess inside.

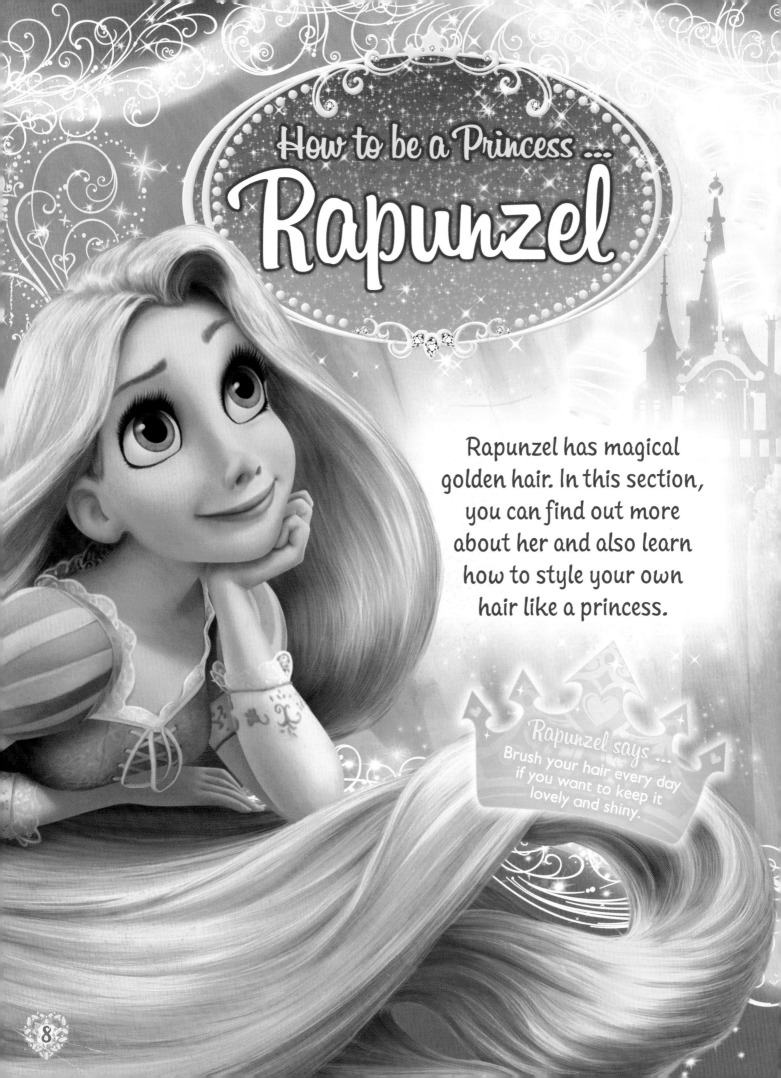

How to be a Princess ...
Rapunzel

Rapunzel has magical golden hair. In this section, you can find out more about her and also learn how to style your own hair like a princess.

Rapunzel says ...
Brush your hair every day if you want to keep it lovely and shiny.

Part 1

Mother Gothel

Mother Gothel keeps Rapunzel locked in a tower so she can use her magical hair to stay young forever.

Flynn Rider

This charming thief is on the run when he stumbles upon Rapunzel's tower. He's in for a surprise when Rapunzel captures him ... with the help of a frying pan!

Pascal

Pascal the chameleon is Rapunzel's first friend. He encourages her to follow her dream and leave the tower where she's lived all her life.

Maximus

This palace horse is on a mission to capture Flynn Rider and nothing will stop him ... until he's befriended by the golden-haired girl.

9

Tower Tale

Find out how Rapunzel escapes from the tower and meets her true love.

Once upon a time, in a faraway land, a queen gave birth to a golden-haired princess. Before the princess was born, the Queen had drunk the potion of a magical flower to cure an illness. But evil Mother Gothel, who had known about the flower's youthful secret for centuries, discovered that she could become young again by stroking the baby's hair!

So she snatched the baby and kept her locked in a tower hidden away deep in the forest. She named the baby Rapunzel.

The King and Queen were heartbroken. Every year, they released hundreds of lanterns into the sky on Rapunzel's birthday hoping that, one day, the lanterns would lead her home.

As Rapunzel grew up, she was never allowed to

tower and decided to hide there. He climbed up and in through the window ... where Rapunzel hit him on the head with a frying pan!

When Flynn came round and swore to Rapunzel that he wasn't there to steal her hair, Rapunzel made a deal with him to take her to see the floating lights that appeared on her birthday. She hid his satchel with the crown inside,

leave the tower. Her only friend was Pascal, a chameleon. Every year, on her birthday, she saw some mysterious floating lights in the night sky. They seemed meant for her. The day before her 18th birthday she plucked up the courage to ask Mother Gothel if she could leave the tower to see them, but Mother Gothel refused her wish.

saying she'd only give it back once he had returned her safely to the tower.

Luckily, Mother Gothel had to go on a journey. As soon as she had left, Rapunzel slid down her hair to the outside world!

In the forest, Mother Gothel came across

Meanwhile, in another part of the forest, a thief called Flynn Rider was on the run from the Stabbington Brothers. He was in possession of a stolen crown. While being chased by the palace guards, and as he desperately tried to get away from Maximus, a palace horse, he stumbled across Rapunzel's

Maximus. Worried
that the guards
had come for Rapunzel, she went back
to the tower and found Rapuzel gone
and Flynn's satchel with the crown and
wanted poster. She now knew who was
with Rapunzel. She set off in pursuit.

Deep in the forest, Flynn took Rapunzel
for lunch. The palace guards found him,
but they escaped through a tunnel.
Mother Gothel had seen everything
through the window though.

Mother Gothel waited until
Rapunzel was alone, then appeared
and demanded she return

with her. Rapunzel didn't want to
leave Flynn, but Mother Gothel said
that Flynn was only interested in the
crown. She dared Rapunzel to give
him the crown.

That evening, Flynn and Rapunzel
rowed to the middle of the harbour
to watch the floating lights and
Rapunzel decided to return the
crown. Flynn spotted the Stabbington
Brothers watching from the shore
and rushed off to bargain with them.
Instead, the brothers tied him up in a
boat and sent him sailing away.

her hair. He climbed up, but Mother Gothel pushed a dagger into his back. Rapunzel pleaded with Mother Gothel to let her save Flynn, but Flynn wouldn't allow it. He picked up a piece of broken glass and cut off her hair! In an instant it lost all of its magical powers. "What have you done?" cried Mother Gothel, as she aged before their eyes. Furious, she ran towards Flynn, but tripped and fell out of the window.

When Rapunzel saw Flynn floating away, she thought he had deserted her. "You were right, mother," she wept, as she was led back to the tower.

But once she was back in the tower, everything started to became clear to Rapunzel. "I'm the lost princess!" she exclaimed.

Flynn had been rescued so he made his way to the tower. When he arrived, he shouted at Rapunzel to let down

Rapunzel was now free and Flynn took her to the King and Queen. Hundreds of lanterns were released into the sky to celebrate her return. Flynn and Rapunzel were soon married and lived happily ever after.

The End

Puzzle Fun

Rapunzel is using her golden hair to escape from the tower!
Can you spot six differences in the bottom picture?

Colour a flower as you spot each change.

Rapunzel says ...
Decorate your hair with flowers and sparkly clips to look as pretty as a princess.

Add some pretty colours to this picture of Rapunzel

Which of these pictures of Pascal is the odd one out?

a

b

c

Crowning Glory

Follow Rapunzel's hairstyle tips to look as pretty as a princess.

Twirly Time

Use curling tongs to create this twirly hair-do. Divide into small sections and fasten with clips.

Princess Ponytail

Wear your hair in a side ponytail for a fun, everyday look. Tie with a ribbon and add flower hairclips.

Glamour Girl

Wearing your hair up looks very glamorous. Add a flower and pretty clips and you're ready for a special occasion.

Flower Power

Finish off your hair-do with fresh flowers. Not only will you look beautiful, you'll smell wonderful too!

Congratulations!

You have learnt all you need to know about royal hair. Colour the heart to complete Part 1.

How to be a Princess ...
Ariel

Ariel is part of a big family and loves being with her sisters ... most of the time! In this section, she will teach you how to show your family that you care.

Ariel says ...
Set aside time to spend with your family. You could play a game, bake a cake or go for a walk.

18

Ariel lives in an underwater castle with her father, King Triton, and her six sisters.

Ariel's friends, Sebastian and Flounder, are like family to her as well.

Ariel is the youngest of the sisters.

Perfect Present

Ariel loves surprising her sisters with handmade gifts. What gift would you make for your family? Draw it in the space above.

Family First

Find out how Ariel saves her sister's wedding day with a kind gesture.

Ariel was very excited because her sister, Arista, was getting married and Ariel was going to be her chief bridesmaid.

Ariel had made her own pretty pink dress and she couldn't wait to wear it. "It's the most beautiful outfit I've ever owned!" Ariel told Arista.

Soon, it was time for Ariel to go to the royal hairdressers to have her hair styled. A friendly octopus brushed Ariel's hair until it shone and attached a pretty pink and orange flower. "This will look lovely with my new dress," Ariel thought to herself.

Ariel sang happily as she swam back to the palace to get ready for the wedding. But when she arrived, she found Arista weeping. "What's wrong?" Ariel asked.

"My dress is ruined!" Arista cried. She explained that she had gone outside to pick some sea-flowers for her hair. When she came back, a group of baby sea creatures were playing chase through the palace.

Worried that the sea creatures might knock over her wedding dress, Arista had shouted at them to be careful. The sea creatures had been frightened by her.

In their hurry to leave, the baby porcupine had accidentally ripped Arista's dress with its spikes.

The baby squid had accidentally squirted ink all over it. The beautiful dress was beyond repair!

"And it's nearly time for the ceremony!" Arista cried. "I won't be able to make another dress!"

Suddenly, Ariel had an idea. "You can wear my bridesmaid dress," she told her sister. "It will go perfectly with the sea-flowers in your hair."

A little while later, the couple were married. Arista looked beautiful in Ariel's bridesmaid dress and Ariel looked pretty in her friend's old party dress.

"Thank you so much," smiled Arista. "I know how much you wanted to wear this dress."

"Family comes first," Ariel said, and gave Arista a hug.

The End

Ariel says ...
Write a song or poem for your family. Copy it into a card that they can keep.

21

Royal Family

Ariel loves spending time with her family.
The seven sisters keep King Triton on his tail!

Ariel says ...
Make your family feel special by telling them how much you love them.

Colour the fish.

Can you find each of Ariel's sisters in the picture? Tick a heart as you spot each one.

22

Magical Makeover

Ariel's sisters have given her a makeover.
Add some pretty colours to this scene.

Congratulations!
You have learnt how to show your family that you care. Colour the heart to complete Part 2.

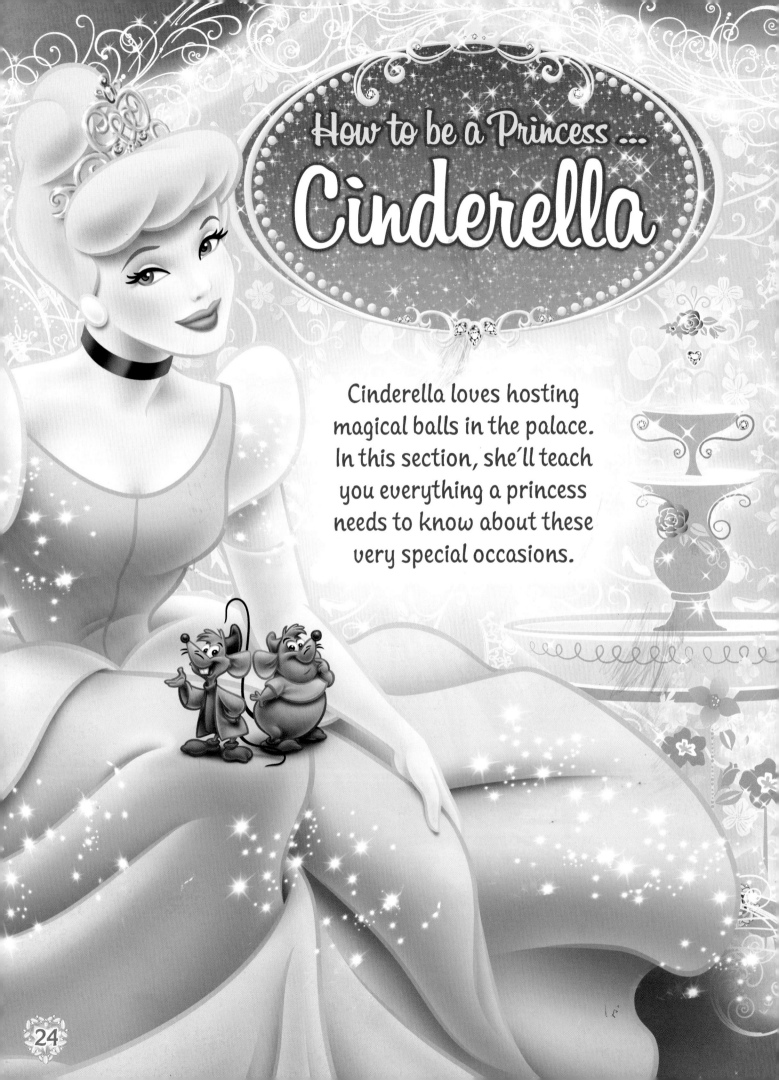

How to be a Princess ...
Cinderella

Cinderella loves hosting magical balls in the palace. In this section, she'll teach you everything a princess needs to know about these very special occasions.

Part 3

Cinderella's fairy godmother used her magic to send Cinderella to her first ball.

The Royal Palace, where Cinderella lives with Prince Charming, has a magnificent ballroom.

Cinderella puts on special balls for her mice friends.

Guest List

mummy   Lily

Princess Ball

Cinderella never forgets a friend when planning a ball. Who would you invite to your ball? Write a guest list opposite.

Cinderella says...
Allow plenty of time to plan your ball so you can make it as special as possible.

25

The Magic Slippers

1 One evening, Cinderella's mice and bird friends were helping her get dressed for a grand ball. Cinderella had made a beautiful new ball gown for the occasion.

2 Gus wanted to make sure Cinderella looked perfect, so he borrowed the Fairy Godmother's magic wand and wished for some glass slippers to match her dress.

3 Cinderella was delighted to find the glass slippers waiting for her in her dressing room. As she arrived at the ball with the Prince, everyone thought she looked wonderful.

4 Inside the ballroom, Cinderella and the Prince enjoyed a dance. But when the music stopped, the magic slippers wanted to keep dancing!

5 Cinderella was confused but the Prince didn't mind at all. "I always love dancing when you're in my arms," he said. The band played another tune, just for them.

6 A little while later, the clock struck midnight and Gus's spell was broken. Cinderella was amazed to see her glass slippers disappear, one by one!

7 Back at home, Gus told Cinderella what he had done. At last everything made sense! Gus promised not to use the magic wand again and offered to polish Cinderella's real glass slipper to say sorry.

The End

Royal Ball

Follow Cinderella's advice to plan the perfect princess ball for you and your friends.

Invitations

Make pretty invitations to send out to your guests. Don't forget to include the date, time and place of the ball.

Music and Dance

Make up some simple dance steps to teach your friends at the ball. Choose music everyone will know.

Ball Gowns
Choose a dress that will make you feel magical. Add sparkly jewellery and pretty hair accessories.

Food and Drink
Ask everyone to bring one item of food or drink to make a feast fit for a princess.

Use your finger to follow the musical trail, then colour in the musical notes!

How many ball invitations can you count on these pages?

Ball Checklist
Tick off each task as you go.

♡ Send out invitations

♡ Choose a ball gown

♡ Make up dance steps

♡ Choose music

♡ Prepare feast

Answer on page 68.

29

To the Ball

Can you guide Cinderella through the maze to her coach?
Don't forget to collect her accessories on the way.

Start

Cinderella says ···
Take photos at your princess ball
and give one to each guest so
they'll always remember
the special occasion.

Finish

Colour the
coach to help
Cinderella on
her way.

Answer on page 68.

Odd One Out

Look closely at the pictures below. Can you circle the odd one out in each row?

1

a   b   c

2

a   b   c

3

a   b   c

Congratulations!

You have learnt how to host the perfect princess ball. Colour the heart to complete Part 3.

Answers on page 68.

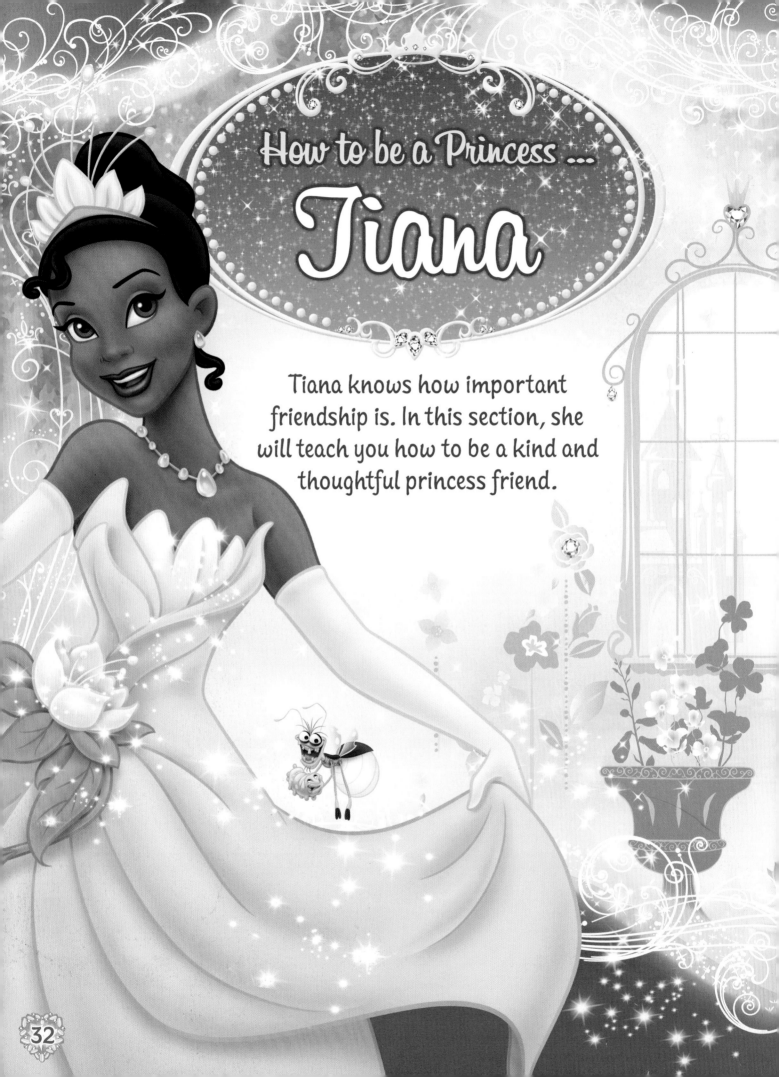

How to be a Princess ...
Tiana

Tiana knows how important friendship is. In this section, she will teach you how to be a kind and thoughtful princess friend.

Part 4

Tiana has been best friends with Charlotte since they were little girls. They share all their secrets.

When Tiana is turned into a frog, she makes friends with Louis and Ray.

True Friendship

Tiana loves Charlotte because she's kind, loyal and lots of fun. Why do you love your best friend? Write the reasons below.

Tiana's new friends help her to become human again.

Jojo Bub

C

P

Good

Tiana says ---
Always be there if a friend needs to talk. A good friend should also be a good listener.

Louis' Big Break

Read the story below. When you see a picture,
use the key below to help you shout out the right word.

 and had been turned into frogs and were on

their way to see , the wise woman of the bayou.

 was telling them about his dreams of playing in a jazz band.

"I'd give anything to jam with the big boys," he said.

"If only you were smaller, less toothy ..." replied , "then you

could play to audiences without scaring them!"

Suddenly, had an idea. "I'm gonna ask to make

me human!"

But  had a better plan. "You can play at Mardi Gras tonight,"

Key

Tiana

Naveen

Mama Odie

Louis

she told . "Everyone will be in costume so they

won't notice you're a real alligator!"

"Oh yeah!" cried , "that sounds good to me!"

 wanted to help her friend. "As soon as we've

been to see , we'll come back to New Orleans

with you," she said. "Count me in!" laughed .

"I wouldn't want to miss this for the world!"

"Little Louis is finally gonna hit the big time!" chuckled .

"Watch out Mardi Gras, here I come!"

The End

Princess Puzzles

Join in the fun in New Orleans by helping Tiana and her friends complete these magical activities.

1

2

3

4

5

Jigsaw Fun

Finish this picture of Tiana and her best friend Charlotte by matching the jigsaw pieces to the correct spaces.

a

b

c

d

e

Tiana says ...
Make a friendship scrapbook for your best friend. You could include photos, letters and drawings.

R V E D S N I A O F

Ray has a message for Tiana. Use the code opposite to work out what it says.

F R _ _ _ _ _ _

_ _ _

_ _ _ _ _ _ _ _

Trumpet Time

Add some happy colours to this picture of Louis playing the trumpet for his friends.

Congratulations!

You have learnt how to be a kind and thoughtful friend. Colour the heart to complete Part 4.

How to be a Princess ....
Aurora

Aurora loves dancing in the woodlands with her animal friends. In this section, she'll teach you how a princess dances with grace and style.

Aurora says ....
Make up dance moves to your favourite song. Keep the routine simple so it's easy to remember.

Part 5

The good fairies love to watch Aurora dance. They wave their wands in time to the music!

Prince Phillip and Aurora enjoy romantic dances in the palace ballroom.

Aurora loves performing ballet in her pretty pink tutu.

Princess Shoes

Every princess needs a pair of dancing shoes! Design your own by adding a pretty pattern to the shoe below.

Sleeping Beauty

1 One day, King Stefan asked Aurora if she could tell her story of 'Sleeping Beauty' to some important palace visitors. "You'll have to read it in your loudest voice," he told her.

2 "Well read, Aurora," said King Stefan at rehearsals. "My guests will be delighted." He was so excited, he didn't notice Aurora looking worried ... she was losing her voice!

40

3 On the morning of the storytelling, Aurora told Prince Phillip she'd lost her voice from talking so loudly. "Perhaps I could tell my story another way?" she whispered.

4 As the important guests started to arrive at the palace, Aurora quickly changed into her ballet costume and the prince laced up her ballet slippers.

5 On stage, Aurora began to dance. The guests were enchanted. Her movements showed her as a young princess. Then, she reached towards the spinning wheel ...

6 ... when she touched it, she stopped dancing and laid down on a bed as if asleep. The audience gasped, wondering whether she would ever wake up.

7 Just then, Prince Phillip danced on to the stage. He leapt to Aurora's side and kissed her. The magic of his kiss seemed to wake her up.

41

8 Then, Aurora danced with Prince Phillip and everyone in the audience clapped. Aurora's beautiful dance had told the fairy tale story of 'Sleeping Beauty' perfectly.

9 "Actions speak louder than words." Aurora said, her voice finally returning, "especially when it comes to true love."

The End

Magical Moment

Aurora and Prince Phillip are enjoying a dance. Colour this romantic picture.

Dancing Fun

Dancing is one of Aurora's favourite things. Follow her top tips to learn how to dance like a princess.

What to Wear

Choose an outfit that you feel comfortable in and shoes that won't hurt your feet. Add a touch of glamour with sparkly jewellery.

Perfect Posture

The way you hold yourself will affect the way you move. Remember to stand up straight, pull your shoulders back and lift your chin.

Time to Smile

Don't forget to smile - dancing should be fun! If you're enjoying yourself, anyone who's watching will enjoy themselves too.

Dancing Duo

Find a dance partner. You'll be able to try out lots more moves if you dance with a friend.

Can you circle five differences in the bottom picture?

Watch and Learn

Watch other dancers to see how they move. You can learn lots from other people, even if their dance style is different to yours.

Aurora loves learning new dances. Tick your favourite dance style below.

♡ Ballet
♡ Tap
♡ Ballroom
♡ Disco

Congratulations!

You can dance like a princess with grace and style. Colour the heart to complete Part 5.

♡

45

Answers on page 68.

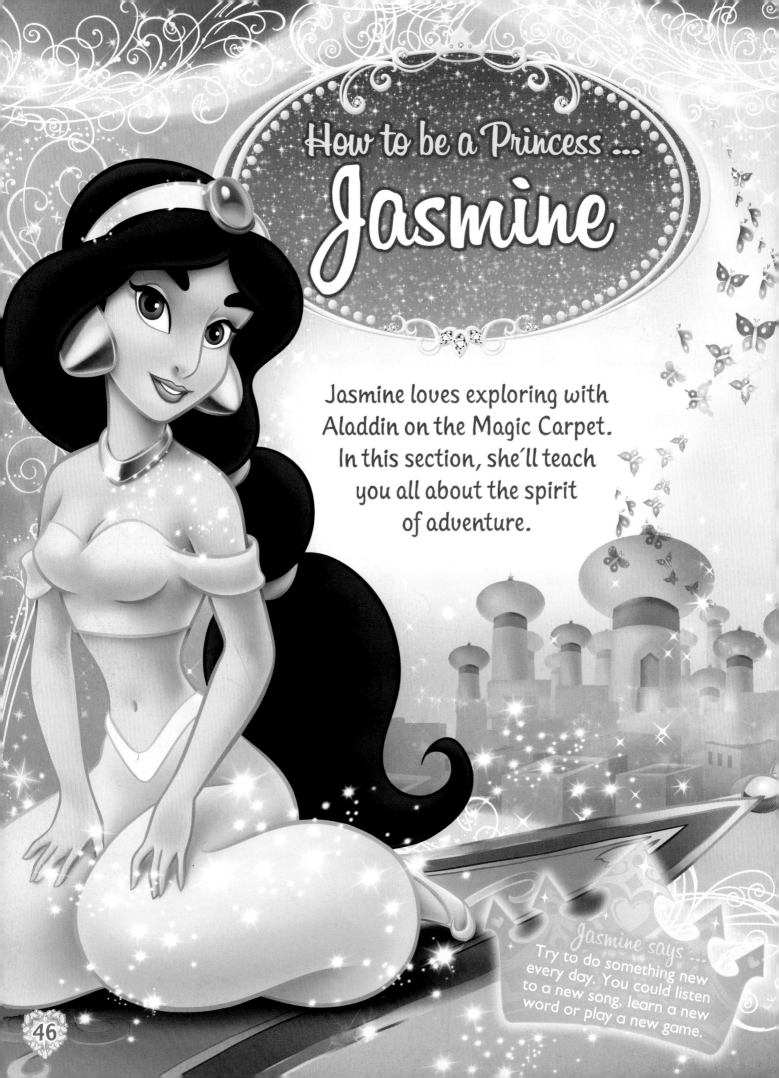

How to be a Princess ...
Jasmine

Jasmine loves exploring with Aladdin on the Magic Carpet. In this section, she'll teach you all about the spirit of adventure.

Jasmine says ...
Try to do something new every day. You could listen to a new song, learn a new word or play a new game.

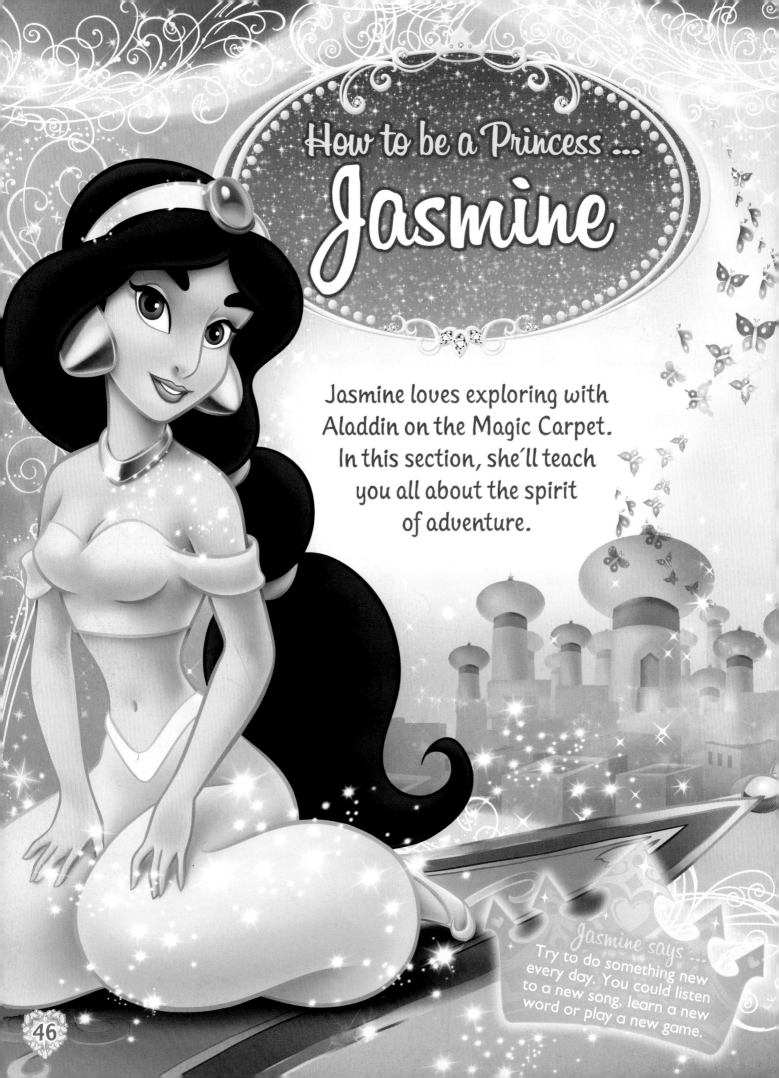

Part 6

Jasmine is brave and adventurous. She always wants to know what's around the next corner.

Jasmine enjoys visiting new places. The Magic Carpet will fly her anywhere she wants to go.

Abu often goes with Jasmine on her magical adventures.

Make a Wish

Jasmine's friend, the Genie, makes all her wishes come true. If you had a magic lamp, where would you wish to be right now? Draw your perfect place in the space above.

Circus Princess

Read this exciting story about Jasmine, the brave circus princess.

Everyone in Agrabah was excited because a circus had come to the kingdom. "I can't wait to see the show," Jasmine told Aladdin as they flew towards the circus on the Magic Carpet. But when they landed outside the Big Top, Aladdin and Jasmine realised that something was wrong.

"It's Allayah, our trapeze artist," the circus ringmaster explained. "She's hurt her ankle and can't perform. We're only in Agrabah for one night and she's our star – without her the show can't go on!"

Jasmine was very disappointed. "I was really looking forward to it," she told Aladdin. "And everyone else in the kingdom was, too."

Aladdin didn't like to see Jasmine so upset. "There must be something you can do," he pleaded.

"The only way is to find someone to stand in for Allayah," the ringmaster explained.

"But she needs to be brave, fearless and adventurous. Where would I find someone like that in time for the show?"

"What about Jasmine?" asked Aladdin. "She's all of those things!"

"Do you think you can do it?" the ringmaster asked. "I don't know," Jasmine admitted, "but I'll give it a try."

They didn't have much time. Allayah quickly told Jasmine all she needed to know. Soon, the Big Top was full and the show was about to begin. Jasmine felt nervous about performing in front of the whole kingdom but she was excited too.

"Good luck," Aladdin whispered, crossing his fingers.

Jasmine climbed onto the trapeze.

The audience gasped as she swung higher and higher. Jasmine moved with such beauty and grace that everyone was hypnotised.

Just then, Aladdin flew up to Jasmine on the Magic Carpet. "You are the bravest, most beautiful woman in the whole of Agrabah," he said, handing her a bunch of flowers. "You're never too scared to try new things and every day with you is a whole new adventure."

The End

Jasmine says ...
Make an adventure scrapbook and fill it with pictures of places you'd like to visit and things you'd like to do.

Jasmine's Wish

Add some magical colours to this picture
of Jasmine making a wish.

Jasmine says ...
Don't just dream about doing
things — make them happen!

Flying Adventure

Which trail should Jasmine and Aladdin follow to reach the moon?

a

b

c

d

♡
Congratulations!
You have learnt all about the spirit of adventure. Colour the heart to complete Part 6.

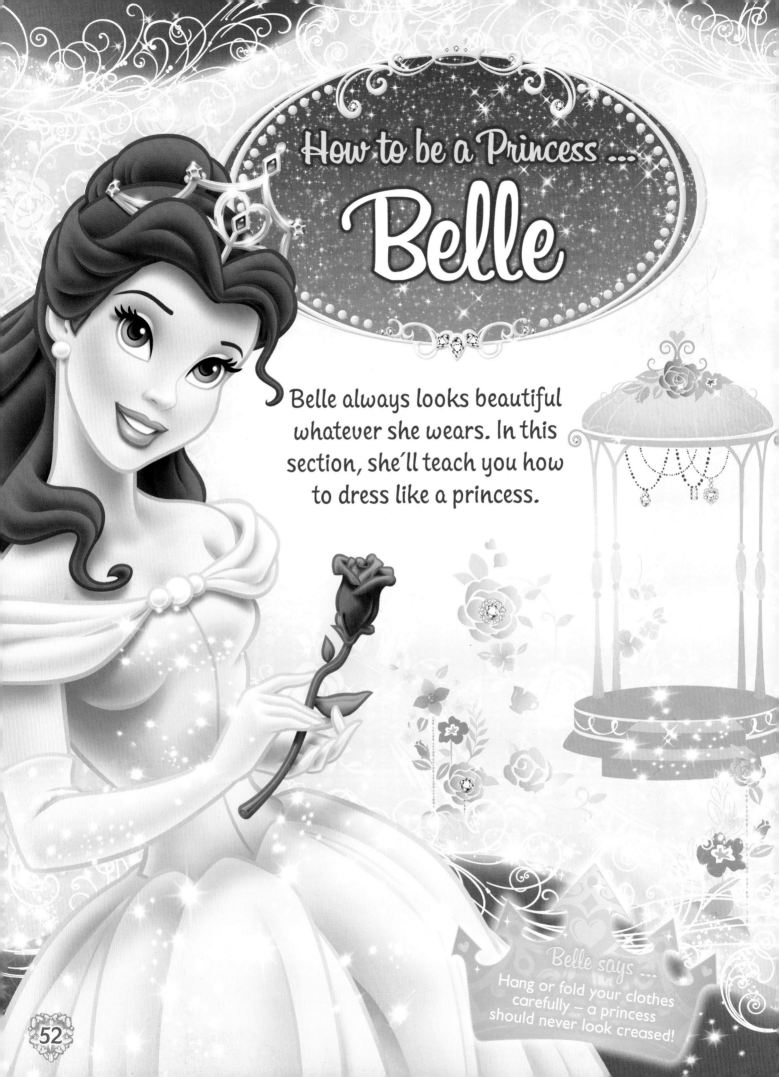

How to be a Princess ...
Belle

Belle always looks beautiful whatever she wears. In this section, she'll teach you how to dress like a princess.

Belle says ...
Hang or fold your clothes carefully – a princess should never look creased!

Part 7

Belle loves dressing up. Her magical friend, the Wardrobe, makes wonderful outfits for her.

Belle's favourite dress is the yellow ball gown she was wearing when she danced with the Beast.

Belle wears long gloves and simple jewellery with her outfits.

Design a Dress

Belle can't decide what to wear! Design an outfit for her by adding a pretty pattern to this dress.

Wardrobe Worries

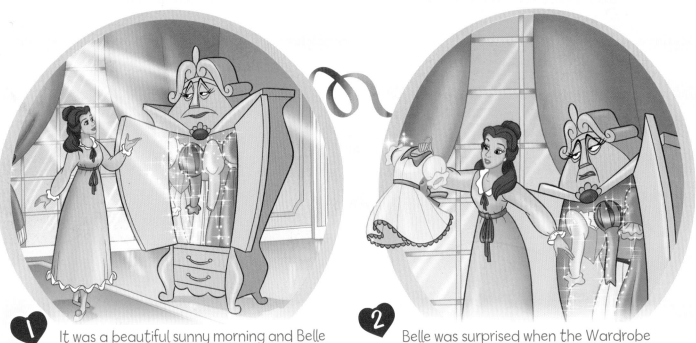

1. It was a beautiful sunny morning and Belle couldn't wait to get dressed. She stood in front of the Wardrobe, wondering what outfit she would give her to wear.

2. Belle was surprised when the Wardrobe gave her a dress that was far too small for her! "I'm sorry, Belle," she said. "I'm feeling worn out today."

3. Belle called her friends together. "We need to inspire the Wardrobe," she told them. "Let's make our own outfits and put on a fashion show."

4. Later, at the show, everyone clapped as Belle appeared in a ball gown made by Lumiere. "I call it 'Dancing Flames'," Lumiere explained.

5 Then, Belle modelled Cogworth's 'Clock Dress' and Mrs Potts' 'Fairy Cake Dress'. Everyone cheered.

6 "This has given me so many ideas." the Wardrobe said, as her doors sprung open and lots of new dresses flew out.

7 Belle had another fashion show. This time, all of the dresses came from the Wardrobe. "I feel like my old self again," the Wardrobe said. "And I love my new outfits!" smiled Belle.

Belle says ...
Make sure your outfit is comfortable to wear. If you feel good, you'll look good!

The End

Royal Dress

The Wardrobe makes sure Belle always looks her best. Follow Belle's style tips to look like a princess, too.

Neat and Tidy

Make sure your outfits are clean and neat – you don't want any marks, missing buttons or frayed edges!

Pretty Accessories

Add a finishing touch to your outfit with jewellery, a belt or a bag. If you want to look like a true princess, wear a sparkling tiara!

Royal Colours

A royal wardrobe should be filled with lots of pretty colours! Pink, blue, yellow, purple and green are perfect for princesses.

Something New

Don't be afraid to try different colours and styles. You might find something that really suits you.

Princess Tiara

Make a pretty tiara to wear with your favourite party dress.

You will need

- Tracing paper
- Pencil
- Silver card
- Scissors
- Sequins
- Jewels
- Glitter
- Glue
- Hole punch
- Elastic

How to Make

Trace the outline above onto silver card. Ask an adult to cut out your tiara and punch a hole in either side of it. Decorate your tiara with sequins, jewels and glitter, then attach a piece of elastic, long enough to fit around your head.

Dressing-up Fun

Join Belle in her dressing room to complete these pretty puzzles.

Gorgeous Gowns

Which dress will Belle choose to wear today? Follow the trails below to find out.

a

b

c

Start

Write your answer here.

58

Tiara Match

Belle has lots of pretty tiaras. Can you draw lines to match the ones below into pairs?

a
b
c
d
e
f

Magical Mirror

Belle is ready for a ball. Add some princess colours to this picture of her looking in her magical mirror.

Congratulations!

You have learnt how to dress like a princess. Colour the heart to complete Part 7.

Answers on page 68.

How to be a Princess ....
Snow White

Snow White found her fairy tale ending when she met the Prince. In this section, she'll teach you the secrets of living happily ever after.

Snow White says ...
Princesses should always be cheerful. Try to think happy thoughts every day.

Part 8

Snow White's wicked stepmother was jealous of her beauty and ordered her to be killed.

Snow White was saved by a kiss from the Prince after she took a bite from a poisoned apple.

The Prince and Snow White lived happily ever after.

Dream Palace

Where would you like to live happily ever after? Draw your dream princess palace in the space opposite.

The Perfect Day

In this story, the Prince gives Snow White some unusual presents.

The Prince was returning from a long trip away and Snow White was very excited about seeing him again.

She cleaned the palace from top to bottom and cooked a wonderful meal to welcome him home.

When the Prince arrived and saw the trouble Snow White had gone to, he held her close. "I'm so lucky to have you," he told her.

The Prince realised that Snow White always looked after him and the Dwarfs, but nobody ever looked after her. "Tomorrow is going to be different," the Prince thought to himself.

The next day, the Prince got up early to cook breakfast before Snow White awoke.

But he left the food on the stove for too long and soon the smell of burning was wafting through the palace. "It doesn't matter," Snow White told him, as she cut up fruit for them to eat instead.

In the afternoon, the Prince took Snow White on a treasure hunt around the palace grounds. But when Snow White found the treasure, she discovered that someone had got there first! "It's not supposed to look like that!" the Prince cried, as Snow White held up a giant heart-shaped biscuit that had been nibbled by a squirrel.

The Prince had a final surprise planned for Snow White and he hoped this one would work out.

"I have a special star to show you," he told her. But when Snow White looked through the royal telescope, she couldn't see a thing. "It's too cloudy," the Prince said, with a sigh.

"I'm so sorry everything has gone wrong," the Prince told Snow White, as he took her in his arms. "I wanted today to be perfect."

"Every single day is perfect," Snow White told the Prince as they began to dance, "as long as I spend it with you."

The End

Snow White says ...
Write a list of things you enjoy – try to do one of them every day.

Happiness Quiz

How much do you know about Snow White's journey to the happy end of her story? Find out with this fun quiz.

1

What poisoned fruit made Snow White fall asleep?

a

b

Snow White says ...
Making other people happy is the nicest feeling. Think of a way to make a friend smile.

2

Who are Snow White's seven friends?

a

b

3

What do the Dwarfs collect in their mine?

a

b

4

Who is Snow White's Prince?

a

b

65

Answers on page 68.

Make a Wish

Snow White is at the wishing well. Complete the activities below before she makes her wish.

3 How many purple birds can you count?

5

1 What is Snow White holding in her hand?

2 A basket

A handbag

2 Can you spot this bird somewhere in the scene?

Congratulations!

You have learnt the secret of living happily ever after. Colour the heart to complete Part 8.

Royal Congratulations

This is to certify that

....
Write your name here.

has become a true princess.

She has shown that she...

Looks as pretty as a princess.

Is kind and thoughtful to friends and family.

Can host the perfect princess ball.

Can dance with grace and style.

Has the spirit of adventure.

Knows the secrets of living happily ever after.

Stick a photo of
yourself here.

67

Princess

Page 14-15
Puzzle Fun

Picture 'b' is the odd one out.

Page 28-29
Royal Ball
There are 6 invitations.

Page 30
To the Ball

Start

Finish

Page 31
Odd One Out
1. c.
2. b.
3. a.

Page 36-37
Princess Puzzles
Jigsaw Fun: 1 - d, 2 - b, 3 - e,
4 - a, 5 - c.
Secret Code: Friends are forever.

Page 44-45
Dancing Fun

Page 51
Flying Adventure
Jasmine and Aladdin
should follow trail c.

Page 58-59
Dressing-up Fun
Gorgeous Gowns: Belle
will wear dress b.
Tiara Match: a and d,
b and f, c and e.

Page 64-65
Happiness Quiz
1. a.
2. b.
3. a.
4. a.

Page 66
Make a Wish
1. A basket.
2. On the well
3. 5.

Just like a Princess

You too can be just like your favourite Disney Princess with the magical collection of playsets from CDI. Baking cup-cakes, playing tea parties, and taking an imaginary shopping trip has never been so much fun!

Disney Princess Magic Rise™ Oven

Bake, decorate and display pretend play treats for your friends. With a wave of the magic wand they'll really rise and come out perfect every time. Then you can decorate them with the pretend icing and toppers which light up with a wave of the wand!

Disney Princess Electronic Bag set

This gorgeous bag contains everything a little princess needs, lipstick, ring a pretty mirror, play money and a debit card. Plus a play mobile friend and car keys that go "Beep Beep" will impress your friends!

Disney Princess Royal Cash Register

Choose a Princess's voice and let her guide you through a magical shopping trip. Includes tiara necklace and a bottle or perfume, plus lots of Play money and a debit card and features a working calculator, debit card swipe, pin machine and microphone.

Beauty and the Beast Talking Tea Set!

Join Mrs. Potts and Chip for tea with this 15 piece set. Listen to the sound of tea boiling when you press the knob on the Mrs Potts' Tea Pot, and chat back to her when she speaks favourite phrases from the film.

The Disney Princess Magic Rise(tm) Oven and Disney Princess Royal Cash Register are available from Argos.

©Disney.